War Cry

BOOKS BY BRIAN MCCLELLAN

WAR CRY

BRIAN McCLELLAN

A TOM DOHERTY ASSOCIATES BOOK

NEW YORK

WAR CRY

Copyright © 2018 by Brian McClellan

Cover art by Richard Anderson
Cover design by Christine Foltzer

Edited by Justin Landon

A Tor.com Book
Published by Tom Doherty Associates
175 Fifth Avenue
New York, NY 10010

www.tor.com

Tor® is a registered trademark of
Macmillan Publishing Group, LLC.

ISBN 978-1-250-17015-6 (ebook)
ISBN 978-1-250-17016-3 (trade paperback)

First Edition: August 2018

The war began before I was born, and for as long as I can remember, someone had been telling us it's almost over.

When I was a kid, sitting in the factories, using my smaller hands to help put together the engine components of our bombers, the radio crackled peace talks half a world away in Ven. I can still recall the newspapers and their inky headlines, when I was a teenager, promising us we were just months away from forcing the enemy's surrender.

And now? Now it's their leaflets, dropped by the millions, coating every inch of our bombed-out cities and pitted wildernesses, telling us to give up because defeat is minutes away. On good days we use the leaflets for toilet paper or to start our cookfires. On bad days . . . on bad days each of us silently considers the offers of amnesty, sees the desperation in the eyes of our friends, and tries to remember the faces of the people we're fighting for back home.

It's early morning as Aleta and I crouch over our tiny campfire, hands practically buried in the flames for warmth while she coaxes the last bit of flavor from month-old coffee grounds. We shelter in the shade of a narrow canyon, cold but safe, and listen to the distant drone of enemy bombers heading toward Bava while the rest of the platoon gets some rest inside the caves we've called home for the last six months.

Aleta takes her pewter pitcher off the fire and sniffs the contents, giving me a hopeful smile. "It'll be good today," she says.

Coffee hasn't been good for years, I want to respond. I bite my tongue. Aleta is twenty-nine, an old woman as far as the war is concerned, and widowed three times over. She can shoot better than anyone in the platoon, and sometimes her cooking actually has some zing to it. Unlike mine. Mine's always shit.

Aleta has earned a little respect. I keep my bitter comments to myself and listen to the distant bombers. I haven't heard the report of an explosion today, which means they're dropping leaflets again.

Aleta can see my tilted head, and cocks her own to listen. "Nine days in a row," she says. "No bombs. Just paper."

"Think they're out of bombs?" I ask.

Aleta shrugs. "We can hope."

"There's always hope," I echo, though I don't feel much. Nine days is a long time to go between bombings, especially when the enemy has the upper hand. I wonder what it means. Last month the radio claimed that the enemy was out of some kind of chemical they used to make their explosives. Who knows? Whatever the cause of their leaflet campaign, I won't argue.

I belong to a tiny platoon of rangers stationed in the Bavares high plains. We protect a vast stretch of scrubland between Bava in the south and enemy territory in the north. There are twenty of us left. Eighteen, maybe? It's been a while since I bothered to count. We have one radio with a broken antenna. From time to time it spits out propaganda, news, coded messages. It goes in and out depending on whether the enemy has managed to bomb our radio towers in Bava faster than we can rebuild them.

We have enough carbines to arm the platoon twice over: a few good rifles, and one machine gun. We have ammunition from the last supply run. We have some fuel for our little one-seater, open-cockpit fighter that the crew affectionately calls Benny. We even have a pilot and a runway, which if the enemy propaganda is to be believed may be the last functioning runway our side controls within six hundred miles.

Our mission is to harass the enemy, to keep them on their toes while the hats back in Bava try to work out a strategy to push them back. We are very good at our jobs. The hats are less so at theirs.

My mind is wandering again, and it takes Aleta several moments to get my attention.

"Teado," she repeats, finally reaching across and tapping me on the shoulder.

I come out of my reverie. "Eh?"

"What are you thinking about?"

"Bread," I lie, giving her a smile. "The kind of bread my mother used to make with the braided dough. Soft like a cloud. Spread with orange marmalade."

"Ach," Aleta responds, touching two fingers to her stomach and falling backwards on her haunches. "You're making me hungry."

I'm making *myself* hungry. She hands me a cup of coffee. It tastes like slightly bitter water, but I thank her because it's hot. Aleta is a good woman, and I think she's been flirting with me.

"Teado," she says.

I look up from my coffee. "Hmm?"

"Did you . . ." She pauses, as if searching for the right words. "Did you have midnight watch at the radio?"

"Yes." She knows I did. The watch roster is written beside the radio. Her face is serious and this puts me on edge. "Did I do something wrong?" I try to think back on the previous night, and wonder why Aleta makes me feel like a schoolboy. Technically, I outrank her. But out here, a platoon of rangers on the enemy line, rank means very little.

She continues on. "I had it after you," she says. "The radio was tuned to enemy propaganda."

I freeze, coffee halfway to my mouth, tongue suddenly dry.

I've spent every night for two weeks hunched over our equipment, earphones pressed against the sides of my head, listening to enemy propaganda during my shift. I try to smile. "Their music is better," I say, waving a hand in dismissal. I hunch closer to the fire, feeling suddenly defensive, hoping she does not prod further.

"Their music *is* better," Aleta says.

This makes me glance up. Back in Bava, listening to enemy propaganda is a shooting offense, and we both know it. "You . . . ?" I ask.

Aleta stirs her pot of coffee and gives a little shrug. "By accident, of course." There is a long, drawn-out silence. I glance furtively at Aleta till she sighs and continues on, "No, not by accident. We all listen, Teado. We all wonder if their food is better, or their beds and clothes warmer. We all look toward the enemy air base and wonder if we could make it there without one of our friends shooting us in the back for desertion."

This admission startles me and makes me feel guilty, all at once. I've been considering those very things for weeks. I'm not sure what to say. She looks me in the eye. "Commander Giado took me aside last month and told me that if any of us makes a run for it while I'm on duty, he would not question me if I miss." She mimes making a rifle shot.

I can hear nothing but my heart beating, and I look

around to make sure everyone is still asleep. This is treason. She has as good as told me that I *could* make it to the enemy if I wanted. I wonder if this is some kind of test, but I think I know Aleta better than that. And she *has* been flirting with me. She wouldn't flirt with someone she might have to kill.

She stares at me expectantly, and I realize that I made up my mind about the amnesty days ago.

"If I took their offer," I say carefully, "they would make me turn over the location of our platoon."

"Likely," she agrees.

"I think . . . I think that I could betray my country. But I could not betray my friends."

This last bit brings a smile to her face, and she reaches out to clink her coffee cup against mine. She gives a happy sigh, and I can sense the issue has been settled. A great weight lifts from my shoulders.

"They really do have better music," I say.

She laughs. "Just make sure you change the radio when your shift is over. We should be a good example for the others."

We fall into a companionable silence. I turn my attention away from propaganda and toward the scorch marks on the canyon walls above us. I can tell by their inconsistent pattern that they don't come from bombs, but rather sorcery, and I wonder what kind it is. The Fire-Spitters on both sides are all dead. There are just a handful of Wormers left in the world. They say the only wizards to survive this long into the war are the Smiling Toms and the Changers.

They've always said wizards would decide the fate of this war. I find it funny, because they're almost all gone.

We're almost all gone.

A third member of the platoon finds her way out into the morning air, sniffing at the faint aroma of coffee. Bellara is sixteen, still chubby-faced despite our inadequate food supplies, and barely five feet tall. Her hands and cheeks are dirty like everyone else's, but her clothes are brightly colored and mostly clean. It's a point of pride with her kind, and we let her have it.

Bellara is a Smiling Tom. Her illusions keep us hidden in these canyons no matter how many scout bikes and flyovers the enemy sends. She hides the smoke of our campfires, the smell of our gas, and even Benny and the runway.

"Coffee?" she asks hopefully, and downs two cups before Aleta cuts her off. We can hear her stomach rumble and Aleta points to the tin of triple-baked biscuits open beside the fire.

"Breakfast."

Bellara checks the biscuits, looks between us and then toward the caves. "How many tins do we have left?" she asks.

"Two," Aleta responds.

Her face is at war with itself. She's desperately hungry—we all are—and since she's keeping us hidden she knows no one will question her for taking a double ration.

Her cheeks twitch, and she takes half a biscuit. "Any sign of Benny and Rodrigo?"

Rodrigo is Benny's pilot. He went to Bava two days ago for supplies and hasn't come back. Maybe he was shot down. Maybe he couldn't find a smooth place to land and had to ditch. Maybe he ran out of fuel. "Nothing," I respond.

Bellara's eyes are a mask, zombie-like. Rodrigo is her brother. She silently heads to the mouth of the canyon to check on her illusions. Aleta and I share a glance, but we remain silent.

One by one, the rest of the platoon joins us. There is muted conversation. Commander Giado is the last to emerge from his sleeping roll, limping along, dragging one gangrenous foot behind him. Giado is a good officer, even wounded and tired. Two weeks ago the town where his wife and child live was all but wiped off the map by an enemy Wormer. He has not smiled since, and I think only his dedication to duty keeps him going.

Harado, our medic, tells us a joke he claims that he dreamt. It's instantly forgettable, but genuinely funny, and gets a few chuckles. Commander Giado snorts, as if exasperated, but I can see the corner of his mouth twitch.

The tin of biscuits is passed around.

I leave Giado and Aleta to talk about a possible raid and follow Bellara out of the canyon, walking slowly, hands in my pockets. The canyon floor is littered with motorcycle parts and empty supply canisters, most of them stolen from the enemy. Selvie has skipped breakfast and gone straight under one of the bikes, trying to repair an exhaust manifold, and I kick her gently as I walk by. She swears at me and asks for a #3 wrench. I find it for her and then continue on after Bellara.

They say that the Bavares is the largest plateau in the world. It is a featureless, inhospitable place covered in scrub brush and devoid of animal life but for the llamas and ground squirrels. The plains are occasionally broken by jutting towers of rock, a spine of mountains that stretch for a thousand miles in either direction. I wonder sometimes why the enemy bothers trying to conquer us, when we live in such a shitty place.

Our platoon shelters in one of the countless canyons that snake through the mountains. We are a few miles from an inactive volcano that makes the air smell like sulfur, and our canyon lets out directly onto the plain where a tiny smuggler's runway provides a safe landing spot for Rodrigo and Benny. It is a risky hiding place, easily discovered by anyone with the air superiority of our enemy—or it would be, without Bellara's illusions.

I exit the canyon to find Bellara sitting in a small cave on the side of the mountain, perched above a forty-foot length of scree. She has taken to sitting there every morning for the last few weeks. It is not a good lookout spot—it faces southeast, without a vantage of either the enemy air base across the plain, or our own tiny runway.

I decide to find out why she likes that spot so much and pick my way carefully around the scree slope. The cave is just a few feet tall and half as deep, and I have to crawl on my hands and knees to position myself beside her. She looks at me sidelong, then sighs, and it occurs to me that perhaps she wants to be alone.

Too late, I'm already here. Bellara tolerates my presence, turning her attention to the scree slope below her. I sit in silence for several minutes, trying to follow her gaze, and am about to ask what she's looking for when a ground squirrel pops its head out of the rocks below us.

It is soon joined by another. They chase each other through the stones, sure-footed, unworried by the occasional shift of the scree. They chatter at each other, one catching the other by the toe, the other nipping at the nose, running and playing. I realize that, despite a cold morning wind blowing across the plain, this cave shelters us both from the wind. It catches the morning sun, warming the rock, and in short time I almost want to take off my old canvas jacket. It is the warmest I've been in weeks.

"Don't tell the others," Bellara says.

"Eh?" I ask.

Bellara nods at the squirrels playing in the scree. "Aleta will want to make them into a stew. She'll set traps, and I'd rather she not."

"They'd be good eating," I suggest cautiously, trying not to let on that the same thought had been going through my mind.

"But they don't deserve to be eaten."

"Does anything?" I ask, laughing.

"Maybe not," Bellara says seriously. "But they're happy. They don't know there's a war on. They don't give a shit about the bombers. I like that. So please don't tell Aleta."

It's the "please" that gets me. Bellara may be just sixteen, but she's been fighting since she was old enough to hold an illusion. She knows her place in the world. Giado is deferential to her. Bombs do not scare her. I don't even scare her, and it took the others several months before they would get close to me. Some of them still keep their distance.

"Okay," I say. "I promise."

Bellara squeezes my hand. "Thank you."

"It's very warm up here," I comment.

"I know. I like that, too."

We listen to the distant bombers for the next half hour. I can hear both our stomachs rumbling, and wonder if it's worth ~~venturing~~ out on the plains to hunt llamas tomorrow. Giado will object, because he's been very cautious since we got word of his hometown. But we could use the meat.

"They say," Bellara broke the silence, "that before the war we were used for entertainment."

"We?" I ask, though I know what she means.

"Wizards. We'd put on shows for hundreds of thousands of people. Fire-Spitters shooting flames toward the moon. Changers dancing in the flickering light. They say Smiling Toms were given leave to create anything they could imagine."

I snort. It seems like such a childish thought. These days Smiling Toms are forbidden from using their strength for anything but the war: stratagems, camouflage, misdirection.

"It's important," I say, repeating a bit of propaganda I heard once, "that we dismiss the childish fancies of our yesteryear, and fight for a better tomorrow." I scowl even as I speak, the words sounding callous. One glance at Bellara's face shows that she disagrees.

"What is more important?" she demands in a gentle voice. "Killing the enemy? Or creating wonder for children?"

"Winning the war," I say automatically, as if the answer is obvious.

Bellara scoffs. "You're right," she admits. "But you're

also wrong." She looks at her fingertips showing through the ends of frayed wool gloves. "I want to create something wondrous. I want to dazzle. I want to make people smile. I don't want to just hide or distract."

"Perhaps," I say, wondering if she's been considering the same offers of amnesty from the enemy, "*that* is the better tomorrow we fight for."

"Then why am I forbidden from doing so now?"

"Because you have to save your strength."

Bellara sighs. "If we allow ourselves no happiness, and we win the war tomorrow, then what have we fought for? We will be a bleak generation on a broken world, and we will never know joy again."

The proclamation seems incredibly poetic from someone her age, though she's only a couple years younger than me.

"Don't you want to dance?" she asks.

"I don't know how," I respond. My mother used to dance when she made bread, but that was a long time ago.

"Is there anyone left to teach you?"

"I don't know."

Bellara spreads her hands, as if to indicate the futility of it all. "I would like to dance," she says. "I would like to create light shows that make children and adults laugh. But no one ever taught me, so if this war ever ends I will be forced to teach myself, and then to convince everyone else that it is no longer taboo." She speaks as if it's a burden that has been placed upon her. Her face is set, stubborn.

I open my mouth to assure her that someday the war will end and she will find someone to teach her. It's a happy lie, as these things go. But a change in the air stops me, and I tilt my head to listen. I shift, crawling out of the cave.

"Where are you going?" she asks.

I point at my ear. "Single engine, flying low."

Bellara's face lights up instantly. "Rodrigo!"

She scrambles down the slope back into the canyon, then around the edge of the mountain. I follow more carefully, then run to catch up when I get on level ground.

The plains to the northeast of our canyon are uneven and spotted with scrub. Narrow gullies dot the landscape, and anyone flying overhead would be hard-pressed to find a proper landing spot within a hundred miles.

The illusion, Bellara explained to me once, was easy to set and maintain. She used her sorcery to mimic a patch of land to our west. Throw in a bit of variance, and no one would ever suspect a runway out here in the middle of nowhere.

Even though I know it is there, I'm not able to spot the runway until I am actually on it. Scrubland turns to old, broken concrete beneath my feet, and forty paces later I see a shimmer of the light. Benny emerges from the morning haze. She is an old red and gray fighter, rusted and worn.

Her engine smokes and whirrs, her propeller looking choppy. There are a few new bullet holes in her wings.

Rodrigo is a small man, not much bigger than his sister. He has olive skin and a frail-looking body, but he is all sinew and muscle like a piece of old leather. He wears a big grin as he climbs down and embraces his sister, and then grabs me and kisses me on both cheeks in greeting.

I look upon Rodrigo's love of flying and his passion for life and realize that my conversation with Bellara was anything but surprising. The urge to perform, it seems, is in their blood.

"Teado!" he says. "I have news. We'll take it to the commander."

"Did you bring back any food?" I try to ask, but I'm cut off by Bellara, who points at the bullet holes in his wings.

"What happened?" she demands.

Rodrigo dismisses her concern with a gesture. "Close call. Some asshole shooting in the air. Nothing to be worried about. Your illusions held well, my sister. I got in and out of Bava." He makes a kissing gesture to his fingers, as if it were the easiest thing in the world. "I was only held up because the garrison captain was waiting for intelligence. Which I have!"

"We could hear you coming in," I tell him.

They both look at me, and comprehension slowly dawns on their faces. Bellara's illusions did *not* hold. The enemy couldn't see him, but they could *hear* him. They hadn't been shooting randomly.

Bellara's face turns ashen. "Rod . . ."

"Shh!" Rodrigo says, putting a finger to her lips. "It's fine. I survived, didn't I? What's war without a little risk? Besides, I'm back and I have news!"

"What kind of news?" I ask.

"Intelligence!"

"What kind of intelligence?"

Rodrigo is evasive the entire way back to camp. Bellara hangs back. I want to comfort her, to tell her we all make little mistakes, but I am too concerned with whatever Rodrigo is holding near his chest.

We interrupt the commander and Aleta, and within moments the whole platoon assembles. We sit on empty supply crates and rocks, or crouch in the dust, Rodrigo, Aleta, Bellara, the commander, and me in the middle.

"I have news," Rodrigo repeats to the commander. His face is stretched in a clever smile, his eyes alight. Rodrigo is one of those loveable fools who lives on the edge between life and death, and I can tell that flying in and out of Bava and being shot at has given him new energy.

Giado chews on the stub end of a cigar that is more mush than paper and tobacco. "Food," he says bluntly.

Rodrigo opens his mouth, looks around at the gathered faces, then leans into the commander. Only those of us closest can hear him. "I brought back ammunition and gas," he says. "Condoms and some newspapers."

"No food?" Giado asks, clearly stricken.

"Two tins of biscuits. Headquarters is straining. It's all they could part with."

The commander visibly struggles to keep his temper in check. "They could spare us bullets and condoms, but no food?" he says in a low voice.

Rodrigo's smile has disappeared. Aleta gets up from her seat to hover, as if ready to swoop in and keep Giado from attacking our pilot. We all know that Rodrigo is simply the bearer of bad news, but the commander has gotten more bad news than any of us these last few weeks, and is clearly at the end of his rope.

Rodrigo hurries on. "There is good news, though. They've given us intel on the enemy."

"Who cares," the commander asks, "if we are all too weak to attack them?"

I reach over and put a hand on Giado's shoulder. He does not look at me, but slumps in his camp chair, tired and angry. "What's the intel?" I ask.

Rodrigo speaks up so that the rest of the crew can hear him. "We've got a target. The enemy has plans for a new air base closer to Bava."

"That doesn't sound like good news," I say.

Rodrigo holds up a finger. "Maybe not for Bava, but it

is for us." He scoots his makeshift seat back and draws in the dust, though only Aleta and I are able to crane our heads to see. "Here is Bava." He indicates a rock. "Here is the enemy's current air base." He draws a line in the sand. "And here is the new one. They've already sent their engineers ahead and have an operational runway cleared. They will begin moving supplies tomorrow at dawn, and the first three cargo planes will be nothing but food."

I stare at his map. The new air base is farther from the mountains, making it harder for us to hit and run. But it also means their new air supply path is closer to our runway than it's ever been before, and well out of reach of their normal patrols. I see Rodrigo's point immediately—their cargo planes will be exposed.

There is an audible silence throughout the platoon. Aleta bites her bottom lip. People grin at each other. Even the commander leans forward, his interest piqued.

"You're suggesting an air drop?" Giado asks.

Rodrigo glances at me and nods.

"We haven't done one of those for four months," Aleta protests.

"That doesn't mean we can't do it again," Rodrigo says.

Aleta shakes her head. "The last air drop nearly killed both Teado and Selvie. We can't risk it."

I swallow, thinking of the possibilities. An entire cargo plane full of rations and equipment could last us out here for another six months. We wouldn't have to depend on Bava for resupply. Hell, if the air drop works there is no reason we can't do it again and again. We've already proved we could operate with impunity—that the enemy's best scouts can't find us. Bellara sees to that.

But Aleta is right. The last air drop *did* nearly kill me. Selvie, too, but when I glance in her direction she's already staring at the sky, talking to herself—probably trying to remember how to fly one of those big cargo planes.

"Can Benny even handle it?" Giado asks. He's talking to Rodrigo, but he's looking at me, and I can tell he's asking for silent permission to give it a try. Headquarters banned air drops last year because they lost too many Changers trying to capture supplies, then lifted the ban when the enemy pushed too far across the Bavares.

"She can handle it," Rodrigo insists. "We'll have to strip her down a bit, but carrying three people won't be a problem."

"Four," Bellara speaks up. "You'll need me to cloak the cargo plane the moment we touch it, or else they'll just follow us back to our base."

Rodrigo's face sours, and it's obvious he hasn't considered putting his sister in harm's way. "What did we do last time?" he asks.

"Last time," Aleta says, "we captured a bomber and landed it in Bava."

Rodrigo chews on his fingernails. "We can't just do that again?"

"We need food," Bellara reminds him, "and if we fly a cargo plane into Bava, headquarters will confiscate the cargo. We'll be lucky to get one crate for ourselves."

"If," I cut in, giving the commander a small nod to indicate I'm on board, "we can take the cargo plane and land it back here, we're set for the rest of summer and most of the winter. I've heard rumors the enemy even has fresh coffee." I don't tell them that I heard that on one of their propaganda broadcasts. No one asks.

Rodrigo shakes his head. "No, no. We'll have to think of something else."

"This is your idea," Bellara reminds him.

"And you're my sister. I'm not taking you up in that death trap."

The rest of us exchange knowing glances while Bellara glares at her brother. On every other day, Benny is his beauty, admired above all lovers. But Benny is relegated to a death trap at the thought of flying his little sister into a mission?

"Benny is not a death trap," Selvie objects. "And I agree, she can carry four people no problem. I'll get to work stripping her down right now." Our mechanic takes off toward the runway before anyone can argue with her.

"I don't think it's a good idea," Aleta says to no one

in particular, watching Selvie go. The objection is half-hearted. She knows as well as any of us that we need supplies, or we will starve.

I glance sidelong at Bellara. Her lips are pursed. She has never objected to, nor volunteered for, a dangerous mission before. I think back on our conversation and wonder if she's going crazy. It is not unheard of for any fighter to become more and more reckless. I myself consider, from time to time, just walking off across the plains.

I let it go, and tell Aleta that I think the mission will be a success. She smiles at me, face hard, having said her piece. The commander's brief moment of awareness seems to pass, and he sinks back into himself, glaring and muttering.

The camp becomes more animated. People smile, and talk in normal voices. Harado repeats the joke he told earlier, and some people laugh out loud. The prospect of a rations coup gets them more excited than any nighttime ambush, and I hear my mention of fresh coffee repeated around the canyon. I go with Rodrigo and Selvie down to the runway to see if there's anything I can do to help to prepare for tomorrow's mission.

———

The next morning proves poor light for a mission. A

cloud cover hangs low over the plains, with dew dripping off Benny's wings as our tiny group gathers beside the cockpit. Rodrigo argues that we call off the mission, but the first hour of daylight quickly burns off the moisture.

Benny has been stripped down to her bare bones, with fuel reserves removed and cargo containers emptied. Selvie removed the seat, replacing it with a plank of wood and an old cushion so that two people can fit behind the stick. She's also wrapped each wing with a pair of leather straps, and the sight of them makes my stomach do a backflip. I tug on the one on the right wing. It *seems* stable.

"It'll be fine," Selvie tells me.

Rodrigo squints into the distance, silently cursing the clearing sky. "Our runway is too short to land a cargo plane," he says in a last-ditch effort to excuse his sister from the mission.

"No it's not," Selvie says. She seems to search her memory, then corrects herself. "The cargo planes the enemy uses are only a little bigger than the ones the smugglers who flew in and out of here used to pilot. Besides, we're not capturing the plane to have a plane. If I run out of runway and shear the landing gear, we still have the supplies."

I turn away from my examination of Benny's wing. This last bit gets me nervous. Not only do I like Selvie, but she's our spare pilot *and* our only mechanic. Lose her, and our jeeps and motorbikes will give up the ghost in weeks. "That sounds like a good way to get you killed," I say.

"Any of this could get me killed," she responds, rolling her eyes.

Commander Giado smells of gin, if you can call what we distill in the back of the canyon gin, but he stands upright through the entire conversation. He looks more like his old self: hard, but fatherly. "This is happening," he declares. "The weather is good and you've got a schedule to keep. Rodrigo, stop waffling."

"Yes, sir," Rodrigo says, ducking his head. He finishes his inspection and helps Bellara onto the wing and into the cockpit, then settles in front of her to start his pre-flight.

Giado shakes my hand and hugs Selvie. "You two take care," he says, speaking louder as the engine roars to life, propeller spinning. "You let Rodrigo circle twice, and if you don't see those cargo planes then come back to base or you'll run out of fuel. Understand?" He's shouting by the end, barely holding his hat on. I nod and climb up onto the wing.

They've given Selvie the warmest clothes they can find. She's wrapped in leather and wool, and I am jealous of how comfortable she looks. I remove my shoes, socks, and jacket, and hand the bundle over to Giado before climbing up onto the wing and strapping myself in. On the opposite side Selvie does the same, checking her counterweights so that my size doesn't unbalance Benny.

The metal is frigid beneath my touch, and I hope I don't freeze to death before the mission is over. My only luxury is an old pair of aviator's goggles.

"Everything okay?" Rodrigo shouts from the pilot seat. I put on my aviator's goggles and give him a thumbs-up, wondering how long it has been since Bellara flew. This mission depends on each of us being able to do all our jobs, and the last thing we need is her passing out or vomiting on her brother's neck. Will she be able to handle her illusions midflight?

As if in answer, the sound suddenly cuts out. There is no sputter of the engine dying, and I can still feel the rattle of the metal beneath me. I hold up my thumb once more, this time for Bellara, as it is her sorcery that has extinguished the sound of Benny's engine.

I worry about Rodrigo's flying, and Benny holding together. I worry about Selvie's ability to fly an enemy cargo plane.

I worry about anything but my white-knuckle grip on Benny's wing and the fact that I am truly terrified of heights. My stomach lurching, Benny begins to taxi.

We're soon in the air and the first couple of minutes are the worst. I stare at the ground off the wing to my right as Benny dips and circles, then watch as it pulls farther and farther away, the scrub brush becoming a blurry, flat sea of pale greens and browns beneath us.

My uneasiness wanes, and I lower my face, pressing my cheek to the reassuring metal of Benny's wing. I stare at the horizon. Despite Bellara's sorcery, I can still hear the hum of the engine through the metal struts of the wing and it lulls me into a sort of tranquil peace. I shiver violently, fighting the urge to close my eyes.

Slowly, careful not to loosen my straps, I pull myself onto my elbows and gingerly look over the top of the wing. I am immediately shocked by how close we are to the ground—no more than a few hundred feet—and wonder if there's been a problem. I glance toward Rodrigo, but his focus is on the stick between his legs. He doesn't seem concerned.

I watch the plain race away beneath us. We're hugging the mountain range, heading north, and soon we begin to ascend. My airsickness returns as we pull up, but I successfully ignore it until I'm struck by the sight of a shadow on the ground behind us. My heart leaps into my throat, and I desperately signal to Rodrigo. There is an enemy plane on our tail, and none of us are the wiser!

I realize my mistake by the time Rodrigo notices me. The shadow I see does not belong to an enemy plane, but to Benny. I breathe a sigh of relief and make my gestures less desperate. I point to Bellara, then at the ground. After several repetitions, Bellara pulls herself part way out of the cockpit and stares toward the ground, then nods at me.

The shadow winks from existence, and Bellara sinks back into her seat.

We slowly peel away from the mountains. The enemy air base becomes clearer in the distance. It looks bigger than our last raid, with nine large hangars and three full-sized runways. Bombers sit lined up beside the runways, looking like toys from so high up. We can see a few of them taking off, heading toward Bava. I wonder if they are filled with bombs or leaflets, and if any of them will return after meeting our anti-aircraft guns.

Rodrigo gives me and Selvie a thumbs-up, and then I feel Benny shake violently as he lets off the throttle. We drop a few dozen feet and I clutch the edge of the wing. We are now barely flying—gliding, more like it—as we wait, invisible, for our quarry. Rodrigo grins like an idiot beneath his goggles.

We are forced to do a full circle around the enemy air base before we see our prey. Twenty minutes behind schedule, I watch as three cargo planes, each of them filled to capacity and wobbling like fat geese, take off from the main runway.

The engine revs, and the world suddenly falls out from under me as Benny descends toward our targets. We halve our altitude and fall in behind them. I watch their shadows on the plain, and glance over my shoulder as the air base fades on the horizon, half expecting enemy fight-

Mississauga Library System
Frank McKechnie Library
905.615.4660
*

ITEMS BORROWED

User ID: 29079820367424

Current time: Mar 21, 2019 6:57 PM
Title: Kill all Happies
Item ID: 39079056888299
Date due: April 11, 2019 11:59 PM

Current time: Mar 21, 2019 6:57 PM
Title: War cry
Item ID: 39079063692676
Date due: April 11, 2019 11:59 PM

Total checkouts for session: 2
Total checkouts: 4

Renew by phone: 905.615.3500
www.mississaugalibrary.ca
Thank you!

ers to come after us.

But we are invisible and silent, and the enemy owns these skies. Why would they bother with an escort?

The enemy cargo planes practically cling to the ground, their pilots still wary of anti-aircraft fire. Rodrigo creeps Benny up behind them, easing us into position with the focus of a cougar stalking a llama. I try to breathe evenly, knowing that my time is almost at hand.

We settle toward the last plane, falling slowly into place until Benny is just fifty feet above her cockpit. Then thirty. Then twenty. Then ten. We are so close that I worry Benny's landing gear will smack their roof. I can see the back of the pilot's head in the cockpit, and realize that if he happened to look up and behind him he might see through Bellara's sorcery at such a close distance.

Rodrigo holds up two fingers. Two minutes. I respond in kind and unlatch one of the straps. Rodrigo holds up one finger. I unlatch the other strap, gripping it with frozen fingers for dear life, knowing that a single slip will send me tumbling a few hundred feet to the hard plain below.

I try not to think about the fall, and focus on the one thing I have complete control over. I take a deep breath, the cold wind catching in my throat. I brace myself on the wing and I *Change*.

My skin becomes leathery, unyielding, though still flexible like the hardest of rubber. Spines grow from my back, slicing through my shirt, creating a parallel set of ridges down either side of my spine. All four limbs elongate and widen, and my back becomes hunched. My fingernails grow into claws, and a long, scythe-like talon grows from each foot like some prehistoric monster. My face broadens, jaws becoming wide and blunt to accommodate rows of razor teeth. Horns sprout from my head.

The entire transformation takes seconds, and I can see Rodrigo fighting with Benny to accommodate the weight of my sorcerous form. He flashes five fingers at me. Four. Three. Two. One. Benny's right wing dips slightly and I let go of the straps to slide down the wing and tumble through the air. I land on the cargo plane's roof with a thud, my talons scrabbling for purchase, scratching at the metal until I'm able to arrest my sliding fall by digging into the seams between rivets.

Every muscle strains as I try to hold on, my heart hammering in my chest, my eyes blurry. It's several moments before I realize that I am perfectly secure and think to wave the okay to Rodrigo above me. He lays off the throttle and Benny slips back behind the cargo plane so my friends can watch my progress.

I dig claws into the rivets, shearing them out like children digging for the meat of a walnut. I get on my knees, using what leverage I can to cut away the metal sheeting with my claws, and then bending back the corners with the strength that only a Changer possesses. Metal squeals as I peel it away.

There is a popping sound. At first I think it's a rivet, then maybe the cargo plane's engine. A second pop is more familiar, and by the third I see the bullet holes in the roof. I'm able to see an enemy: a bright-faced, scared-looking man with a pistol, shouting frantically toward the cockpit. I reach through the hole and snag him through the wrist with a single claw, jerking upwards to slam him against the roof of the plane, and then dropping his body. My claws come back slick with blood. I finish carving an opening and drop down inside.

The plane is loaded to the ceiling with supplies. I take a moment to wonder at all the medicine and gas and rations, my stomach letting out a gurgle despite the adrenaline rushing through my veins.

There are five men inside. One is already dead, his neck bent at an unnatural angle, his arm bleeding all over a tin labeled "desert rations." A second draws his pistol and fires at me. My ears ring from the sound of the shots. Bullets slam into my chest, driving me back a half step but having no more lasting effect to my sorcerous skin than a toy pellet gun.

I cut off his gun-hand at the wrist with my claws while the copilot unbuckles. Through the ringing in my ears I can hear the pilot screaming into the radio. There's a sudden gust, nearly knocking me off my feet as the third guard opens the side-loading cargo door. I spin to him, only to receive the heavy end of a fire extinguisher to the bridge of my nose. Dazed by the sound of the gunshots I clutch for some kind of purchase as the copilot kicks at my legs, trying to get me to fall back through the cargo door.

I rise to my full height, bracing myself against the roof, and snatch the copilot by the head, his face fitting neatly in the palm of my hand, and fling him out the cargo door behind me. The third guard struggles to load a submachine gun, and I take it from him and grapple him toward the door. We both slip and slide on the blood, but I dig into the metal with my talons and throw him after the copilot.

I catch sight of something outside the cargo door and see that Rodrigo has brought Benny up beside me. I realize the change of plans as Selvie unbuckles and shakily gets to her feet. I move quickly to the cargo door, setting my talons and one clawed hand, and reach out with the other. In a burst of courage I know I would lack, Selvie lets go of the securing straps and sprints down the wing, leaping toward me. I snag her one-handed from the air, careful not to dig in with my claws, and bring her safely inside.

She pats my chest, her face flushed, as I set her down. Outside the cargo door I can see Rodrigo cackling like a fool, and Bellara peeking up from the cockpit beside him. Benny pulls away and blinks out of existence as Bellara's sorcery conceals her.

"There's still the pilot!" I shout into Selvie's ear, pointing toward the cockpit. She reaches for her pistol, but I see a sudden panic in her eyes. I toss her deeper into the cargo plane, turning to face whatever gunfire the pilot is about to unleash on me, but am suddenly slammed into from the side.

The pilot is a big man, muscled and fat, and clearly used to a brawl. His punches do less to me than the bullets from his comrades, but he leans his weight into me, bullheaded. I stumble back, my talons no longer catching purchase on the floor, and reach for something to steady myself.

There is nothing there.

I windmill once, managing to snag the pilot by the front of his shirt as we both tumble out the cargo door. My confidence is suddenly undone. There is nothing solid beneath me, beside me, or above me. I am falling, trembling, with only an enemy to hold on to.

The last thing I see before I hit the ground is Selvie's stricken face poking out of the cargo door.

———

A few-hundred-foot fall does not kill a Changer. It hurts. It hurts like hell. I am frozen with indecision and fear as my brain regains control of my body. I can still hear the drone of the cargo planes in the distance, so I have not been unconscious long. I twitch a finger, experimenting, then move my wrist.

My pelvis is shattered, I think, but I can still turn at the waist. I am convinced I have broken an ankle, but it bears my weight without wrenching a scream from my mouth. Slowly my body begins to obey my commands again.

I lie halfway in one of the small fissures that crisscross the plains, and I am covered with blood. For several minutes I worry it's mine and search for my wounds. It isn't long before I find the enemy pilot nearby. Or what's left of him. The fall killed him instantly, I am glad for that, because I have had to put men out of their misery before.

Unsteadily I gain my feet, searching the horizon. I spot two cargo planes in the distance, watch as they turn lazily through the air, heading back to the air base, no doubt worried about another enemy attack. I do not see Benny or the captured cargo plane, and wonder if Selvie has managed to take her home. There are no plumes of smoke in the sky, so she has not crashed. I can only assume that everyone has done their jobs well.

Everyone except for me. I try to clean myself with the tattered remains of my shirt, but give up when I realize that the enemy cargo planes will come back overhead. I climb back into the fissure and lie still, hoping that they take me for dead and report the loss.

I lie caked in the blood of the pilot for most of the afternoon. Enemy aircraft crisscross overhead. They are looking for the stolen cargo plane, I tell myself, though there is a small part of me that is certain they are looking for me. I hope they do not bother to send a ground scouting party and pass the time by thinking of all the supplies in that plane and the look on Aleta's face when she gets some proper food to cook.

The patrols leave off by seven in the evening, and I allow myself to clean off the dried blood. I know I should leave the pilot where he fell, but I am struck by his bravery. Not a lot of men would charge a Changer barehanded, and for that I bury him in one of the fissures and cover his body with rocks. Though I am in pain from the fall, it is a simple enough task in my Changed form.

I even say a prayer from my childhood, though the words mean little to me.

Using the mountains as guideposts, I estimate that I am some thirty miles away from our little guerilla runway. The plains are not easy to cross on foot, even for a Changer, and I know it will take me several nights to return home without a motorbike. I wonder if Rodrigo will come looking for me, and dismiss the notion.

Even if he could spot me, he would not be able to land to pick me up.

I begin the long trek as night falls. I head west, toward

the mountains, until I have reached foothills that will shelter me from searchlights and patrols. These few miles are all I can manage this first night. It will take me much longer to reach camp than I thought. I am not dead. My body is not irrevocably broken. But not even a Changer can fall from a plane and come through unscathed.

For two nights I limp north through the foothills. Everything hurts. During the long periods of darkness, eyes focused on the ground in front of me to keep my footing, I am assailed by doubt. What if Selvie never made it back with the cargo plane? What if Rodrigo and Bellara were shot down on the way home? What if the whole platoon has written me off, said a few words, and moved the camp?

It would be smart of them to loot the cargo plane and then retreat farther into the mountains. They could re-group and regain their strength, and be ready to fight again within weeks. It's the intelligent option, and I know that if they take it I may never find them again. Bellara's skill at illusions works both ways—if the enemy cannot see them, then I will not be able to track them down, either. I will make it back only to return to an empty camp.

My Changed form protects me from the elements and lets me travel faster than a human, but I grow weak from hunger by the fourth night. There are tiny foods along way: edible scrub grass and tubers. They are not enough. I find the recent corpse of a llama and eat my fill, not daring a fire.

I vomit it all back up half a mile later.

On the fifth night I am overcome by thirst. I know the high plains as well as anyone raised on the Bavares, but even I have a hard time finding water. I begin to see flashes of light in the mountains, and know that the delirium has set in. I decide I can push myself another two nights before I am unable to continue on, and I console myself by imagining the feast that must have accompanied Selvie's return. It is a cruelty to my stomach, but the thought of my friends' celebration helps calm my pangs of doubt.

I sleep by day—what sleep I can get on the cold ground—by huddling in the broken valleys of the foothills. A snake joins me for warmth, and I manage to kill it and have my first real meal in days. I keep it down. The blood is warm, the flesh tender.

During the long nights I reflect on my nature. I have been Changed for days, longer than I've ever maintained this other form. I am a reptilian monstrosity crawling across the scrubland. Am I even human anymore? I wish had gone to a university. The universities are all but gone, of course, but ah, how would it have been to study philosophy? To stare up at the sky and ponder on the source and essence of what makes me what I am, to Change and observe that Change, to study myself and others like me. Now there are almost none of *me* left.

I wonder if Bellara will ever bring joy with her illusions, and if she'll think of me when she learns to dance.

I am halfway through the eighth night, still traveling on a belly of raw snake meat, when I decide that the lights in the mountains are not a delirium. The feeling of being watched, that sixth sense that animals have had since creation, hits me like an enemy jeep. My skin crawls and if I had hair on the back of my neck in my Changed form, it would have stood on end. I stop to sniff the night air for some hint of humanity. I pick up a whiff of gas, but I cannot be certain.

For the next couple of hours, the feeling of being followed grows within me. My Changed sight is not a perfect night vision, but I see figures on the ridges. Wolves? There haven't been wolves in this part of the Bavares for thirty years. Mountain lions do not hunt in packs.

As daybreak approaches I realize that I am closer to my platoon's hidden runway than I could hope. Six, maybe seven miles by air? Overland is a range of mountains between me and my friends. If they are still there.

I pause at a crossroads only I can see. The shorter way is through the plain. If I push myself, I think I can be back to camp in less than two days—but that would require traveling by day across the open plain, where I would be obvious to enemy flyovers.

I hear the droning of their bombers every day, see the

cargo planes passing overhead. The cargo planes have escorts with them now, and I tell myself it's because our raid was successful, but my happiness at the thought is short-lived. They are still moving forward, setting up their air base and creeping closer to Bava.

The longer way back to camp is to go over the mountain. It is a shortcut, as the crow flies, but the terrain is rough. It will take me three days or more, but I know where to find water and wild mushrooms.

I make camp, my mind still not made up, sleeping restlessly through the day, worried about being seen. When night falls I make my decision and head into the mountains.

My unseen followers seem to flank me as I navigate the crags and slopes of the goat trails. Sometimes I think I spot them by the light of the moon—human-like figures, a little too large and grotesque—but I do not trust my own senses after so much effort on so little food and water.

I now think they are Changers, but the idea makes no sense. I have seen at least three separate creatures, and Changers do not gather in such numbers, not since far earlier in the war. They are too valuable, spread out across squads like mine in both our forces and the enemy's.

Could they be runaways? Some sort of war-weary coalition hiding here in the mountains? Are they enemy Changers, come together to hunt my friends? The first thought exhilarates me. Both scare me.

I try to move quietly, to somehow lose them, but my talons drag along the rocks. My body sags. I wonder how much of a fight I can muster if they decide to attack. I have no hope against three Changers, but I have fought my kind before, and decide that I can take one of them with me even if they come en masse.

Considering strategy helps me focus, pushing onward up the narrow trail. Rocks tumble from a ridge to my left as a figure maintains my flank.

They know I am here. They must know that I know they are also here. Am I being herded toward an ambush? Am I being observed? Am I being escorted out of their territory?

I shake my head at the last. It is too feral. I am a Changer, not an animal. Perhaps I have been Changed for too long, back hunched, legs elongated, traveling only by night.

I stop and sniff. Petrol on the wind again. This time I am certain of the smell; just as certain as I am that I am being followed by wizards.

A brief fear seizes me. If there are Changers in the mountains, there might be other wizards. If I am being tracked by a Smiling Tom, I might be a dozen miles off course and wandering farther into the mountains. I try to think of a motivation for leading me astray, and the explanation is easy: they want me dead without a fight.

I try to recall what Bellara taught me about seeing through an illusion. The key, she has said, is to trust all of your senses together. The very best Smiling Toms can fool smell, sight, hearing, and even taste. They cannot fool touch, and even an expert will struggle at fooling all of the senses at once.

The path I follow *feels* familiar. The smells—besides the distant whiff of petrol—are of the mountain flowers, the stone, and the dirt. I decide that I am not being led astray.

I continue on for several hundred more yards before I crest a slope, only to spot a Changer standing some ways down the path. He—or she, I decide—is smaller than me. Her talons dig nervously at the dirt, and she has a hooked beak instead of a jaw, and spiraling horns that remind me a bit of fanciful art I once saw of a satyr. She seems startled to see me so close and scrambles behind a boulder.

I stop, looking behind me. Another has been trailing me. I can't quite place the third.

I am tired. The moon is only a sliver, and I do not want to pass that boulder. She will be close enough to touch, a perfect ambush. A small part of me—the human part—wishes for a machine pistol, though I know by experience it will do little but annoy my adversaries.

I stare hard toward the boulder the Changer is hiding behind and then limp over to a nearby rock. I close my eyes, focusing inward on my sorcery. I reverse the joints on my arms, force the claws to recede from my hands and the talons from my feet. Spines shrink and disappear. In a few moments I am human again, and immediately I feel the bite of the cold night air. I am all but naked, clothed in the tattered remnants of the pants I wore for the air drop mission. I sit on the rock and throw up my hands, trying to look relaxed.

In reality, I am tense. I can Change in a moment, talons striking, teeth tearing. I hope that they cannot see that tension in the darkness.

I wait for five minutes, then for ten. I hear stones turn in the darkness. It feels good to rest, but I can feel myself slipping away. A figure scrabbles across the scree to my right, just over the ridgeline. It passes me, going up the path, and then I see it dash behind the boulder where the first Changer has hidden.

If I strain, I think I can hear a whispered conversation.

"Javiero!" a woman's voice suddenly calls out from the darkness.

I turn and watch as a Changer charges up the path from behind me. He reaches the top of the slope and, seeing me sitting less than a dozen paces away, stops. Like the first Changer, he is smaller than me. He has hooked spines on his elbows and leathery skin covered in old scars. I realize with a start that he is naked, and wearing a satchel on his back. I would laugh at the silliness of such a creature wearing a backpack, if it wasn't such a good idea—a good way to keep your clothes from being destroyed every time you Changed.

The Changer—Javiero—paces back and forth along the path, blocking my retreat and glaring past me. A few long moments pass and I hear the crunch of gravel under foot. Wary of Javiero, I glance toward his companions.

I am surprised to see a man and a woman emerge from the darkness. They have Changed into humans. The man shrugs into his jacket, while the woman levels a submachine gun at me. Her face is thin, elfin, her features delicate. She looks like she's in her thirties, but I can't be sure in this light. Her finger floats around the trigger of her weapon.

"What are you doing, Marie?" Javiero asks in a guttural tone.

Marie does not answer him. Her submachine gun does not waver as they draw closer. The unnamed man is bigger than his companions, almost as big as me, and I spare a glance for their clothes. Both of them wear old, beaten leather jackets, but they are in good repair. The man's has no emblems. Marie's has the patch of the Bava city militia on her shoulder.

Marie, Javiero: these are names that belong to my people. Her Bava city militia jacket confirms it, but I am still apprehensive. Three Changers up here in the mountains on their own could mean anything, and I wonder again whether they are runaways.

If they are, they will kill me to keep their location hidden. It is what I would do.

"Who are you?" Marie demands.

I try to look tired, beaten, slumped on my rock. Inside I consider which to kill first, and worry that I cannot Change before her bullets rip my human skin to tatters. "I could ask the same of you," I say.

"But you don't have a gun."

I shrug. "Makes no difference to me."

Her hand tightens on the submachine gun, and I curse myself for the implicit threat. But I have dedicated myself to a role, and I must stick to it. I glare at her glumly, forcing myself to ignore the Changed Javiero still fidgeting behind me. I am the man too tired to care whether he lives or dies, and it is not a hard act to accomplish.

"Let's kill him and be done with it," Javiero suggests.

I continue to ignore Javiero. He is obviously not in charge. "Marie?" I ask. "You are from Bava?"

Marie does not move. The man beside her approaches me slowly. He holds his hands in the air, like an animal keeper trying to free a feral cat from a trap. I hold still, allowing him to check my tattered clothes.

"His belt," the man reports, "is the kind given to Bava rangers. Pants, too." He backs away from me as cautiously as he came.

"Deserter?" Marie asks. The question is not unkind, and it is directed toward me.

I tighten my jaw, realizing this is not a bluffing game I can win. "I could ask the same of you."

Marie snorts. "We have no interest in deserters, but you can't pass this way. Go back the way you came and we won't kill you." She lowers her gun and turns away from me, heading up the path while her two companions still regard me with suspicion.

I still wonder who they are. The regular military would execute me on any strong suspicion of desertion. Other deserters would not allow me to live, unwilling to risk me taking their location back to Bava. I dare to hope that I have stumbled on a friendly platoon, and I take a gamble. "I'm not a deserter."

Marie scowls at me over her shoulder, crosses her arms. "Prove it."

I search for a way to do that, but my mind is sluggish. "I'm a Changer," I try.

"Changers desert," Marie says.

"I am . . ." I hesitate to give my name and rank, as I realize that those won't help. Anyone can desert. "How long have you been up here?" I ask.

Marie's eyes narrow in suspicion. "Why?"

"Have you picked up an enemy mayday recently?"

Marie shakes her head, but her companion touches her on the elbow and gestures for me to continue.

"A week ago—no, nine days ago—we air dropped on

an enemy cargo plane when they started to move their air base up. They got off a mayday before we were able to secure the plane."

"And what happened to you?" Marie asked.

"Their pilot sacrificed himself to knock me out the cargo door."

"Nobody tries air drops anymore," Javiero growls, reminding me of his presence. He's moved closer, and I try not to tense. "We have no planes, no pilots, and no runways."

"Rodrigo is my pilot."

Marie raises her eyebrows, the muzzle of her submachine gun twitching. For a moment I think she will shoot me, and then she laughs. "Rodrigo. Only that son of a bitch is crazy enough to try an air drop with one of our last working planes." She purses her lips. "He's with the Vicuña Platoon, correct? You have both a Smiling Tom and a Changer, which makes you . . ." She seems to search her memory. "Teado."

I'm surprised she knows my name. "That's me."

She glances at her companion. He says, "The story checks out. The mayday said a Changer was on board. And if it was Rodrigo . . ."

Marie shoulders the strap of the submachine gun, letting it fall by her waist. "Stand up," she tells me.

I allow myself to relax for the first time in over a week

and climb to my feet. If they are going to shoot me, I decide, they would have already. There is a niggling doubt in the back of my head but I ignore it. I am too tired, too hurt, too alone to care. They are from Bava and they seem friendly, and I decide I will go with them even if it means my death.

"I am Marie," she says, then gestures at her hitherto unnamed companion. "This is my cousin, Martin. Behind you is Javiero."

I shake hands with Marie and Martin. Javiero ignores my offer. He shoves past me and heads up the path with a grunt, stalking along, still Changed. I watch him go, before turning my attention back to Marie.

"You've been heading north," Marie says. There is an implicit question and I decide on a show of good faith.

"Returning to my platoon. The airdrop was quite a long ways from here. I've been walking since."

She gestures for me to follow, and I fall in just behind her as we work our way up the mountain path. "Do you still have a long ways to go?"

"Six or seven miles how the crow flies," I say. I curse myself silently, frustrated that I gave away our hidden location so easily. I should be more suspicious, even with friends. "Where are we going?"

"To our camp," Marie responds. "We can give you one night succor, and supplies to see you back to your platoon."

Rocks turn beneath my bare feet, and goose bumps form on my skin. I remember how soft and vulnerable it is to be human. Luckily I am not so removed from my childhood on the Bavares that I cannot walk barefoot in the mountains.

"Who *are* you?" I ask, jerking my chin toward the dark figure of Javiero up ahead. "I've never seen three Changers together before."

"Special mission," she replies. "Special circumstances. I'll let Commander Paco tell you about it, if he thinks you need to know." She hums to herself absently, then continues. "I'm surprised you made it this far. That new air base close to Bava has them running patrols all day, and they've even got a functional road."

"Are you here to destroy the new air base?" I ask, even though I know we are far to the north of the base. I am immediately suspicious of conflicting orders, and hope that we—my platoon, and this special group—are able to stay out of each other's way.

"I'll let Paco explain," Marie says.

Before I am able to press further, we reach the top of a ravine and pass over a ridge, and I am suddenly struck by a vision I did not expect this far into the mountains.

In the valley below us is a camp. It is much larger than Commander Giado's camp, easily four or five times the size. I count sixty motorbikes and dozens of tents before I give up.

Martin taps me on the shoulder, and I realize I have stopped in the middle of the path.

It's been years since I have seen so many soldiers in one camp, and that was back in Bava—not here in the wilderness, pushing back at the enemy's foothold in the Bavares. There are cookfires, and the sound of generators, and electric lights. I see several mechanics working through the night in one corner of the valley. I am speechless.

"You have a Smiling Tom," I say, watching the way the smoke from the cookfires disappears as it reaches the top of the ridge.

Marie nods, tight-lipped. I find my feet and follow her down the narrow incline into the valley. Now that I think to look for them I note tire tracks in the gravel at my feet, and I wonder how such a large venture—moving so many men up here into the mountains—was not reported to us when Rodrigo visited Bava over a week ago. Hell, they could have sent us a coded message to expect reinforcements. It would have raised morale something fierce.

We enter the camp. The few cooks and mechanics out at this time of night stare at me curiously, and I am suddenly more conscious of my bare skin and shredded clothes. Marie disappears into a large, dark tent in the center of camp. I can hear whispers, and she reappears a few moments later with a nod. "Commander Paco will meet you in the morning," she says, "but he says to give you a tent and something to eat. I think we can find you some clothes, too. He's pleased that you're a friendly."

I note that Martin and Javiero have fallen back, but are still watching me. There is some trepidation to their gazes. I try to ignore them. "How did you find me?" I ask Marie.

She leads me farther into the camp, over to the edge of the ravine beside a steep bit of scree. It's close to where two mechanics work loudly on a disassembled motorbike by a floodlight, a generator rumbling beside them. Marie says, "Scouts spotted you two days ago. It's not often you see a Changer heading across the plains at night, so Commander Paco told us to keep close if you came this direction."

I think about my decision back at the foot of the mountain, wondering at my stroke of luck. Without the turn into the foothills I might have been sleeping out in the open again, hungry, cold. A real sleeping roll and a bit of gruel sounds like heaven to me.

Someone calls out Marie's name from across the valley. She scowls in that direction, looking suddenly distracted, and indicates a nearby tent. "This belongs to one of our scouts. He won't be back until tomorrow afternoon, so feel free to use his sleeping bag." Her name is called again. "You have about five hours until everyone is awake. Sorry about the generator, but we only have so much room here so the mechanics have to work round-the-clock. Try to get some sleep."

I'm about to ask after the promise of food, but Marie turns and strides back toward the command tent without another word. I stifle my annoyance, realizing I'm lucky to have a warm place to sleep at all, and crawl inside.

The bedroll is flat and uncomfortable, but it is better than the open plain. I lie on my back, unable to sleep, the sound of the generator grating on my nerves even though I have slept through bombing runs since I was a child.

A bundle is thrust into the tent without comment half an hour later. There are new clothes that prove a proper fit, if a little big, and an individual tin of army rations inside which I find biscuits, cheese, even tuna. I revel at the small luxury, eating slowly. I am wide awake now, and my mind turns these events over and over again in my head.

My platoon has been six months on the Bavares without backup, and only the barest supplies out of Bava. We have lost half our number during that time, but we have also done disproportionate damage to the enemy. I've always thought of us as valuable—indispensable, even—and told myself that we have received so little from Bava because they have nothing to give.

Yet here I find an immense camp of friendlies. There must be over a hundred and forty soldiers here, an army by our guerilla standards. They have motorbikes, mechanics, at *least* three Changers, and a Smiling Tom. This is a major operation.

Why not tell us about it? I'm a soldier, so I am used to being kept in the dark by the higher-ups, but this seems silly.

I stare up at the ceiling of my borrowed tent, fingers laced behind my head. The new clothes feel awkward, and I realize I hope that Giado has kept my old, ratty ranger's jacket safe. I wonder if Marie's superior officer, this Commander Paco, will let me take some rations to my platoon. I'm still not completely certain that we succeeded in the hijacking of that enemy cargo plane.

My mind keeps wandering back to the purpose of this little army. Marie did not answer my questions, but indicated I may get answers in the morning. I consider possible stratagems, trying to predict the orders that have found such a large group out here hidden in the mountains, and lay out the facts in my head:

We are, for all intents and purposes, behind the enemy line. This is the biggest friendly army I've seen in years. They have hidden up here for at least eight days—long enough to have heard the mayday of the cargo plane me and Selvie captured.

If they are here to mount a full-scale attack on the enemy, why did they not do it when the enemy was most vulnerable, back when they were moving their operation up to the new air base?

I leave my tent, troubled. No one has asked me to remain in quarters, and with my new clothes the few people awake at this hour ignore me. I am able to walk freely throughout the valley.

The freedom feels comfortable, like I'm back with my own platoon where we sleep and wake when the need arises and nothing stands on ceremony. But I remember the training I received as a boy and I know that this is not how a real army behaves. There should be military police, night watch, proper shifts. As a Changer I should have already met the quartermaster and commander. I should be apprised of current orders. I am technically an officer. After so long behind enemy lines, these realizations come back to me slowly.

There are several supply tents, and I am shocked to find them packed full of crates. Ammunition, weapons, grenades; tins of crackers, meat, cheese, biscuits, and even cookies. There is enough in just a few supply tents to keep an army this size moving for over a year. I lick my lips, and my face grows hot as I remember Rodrigo returning with just two tins of biscuits.

All the army could spare, was it?

I am confused now, and more than a little angry. There is so much I can't explain, and the pieces that I do have don't seem to add up.

I look around for a familiar face, but do not see any of

the three Changers that brought me in. I find one of the mechanics working near my tent.

"Do you know where I can find Marie?" I ask.

"At this time of night? She's either in her tent or with Paco," the mechanic responds without looking up.

I cross the valley, looking on the camp with new eyes. It is too casual, too slapdash. I do not know where Marie is bunking down, but I want answers now, and I decide that I will have them even if I have to wake the commander.

Commander Paco's tent is no longer dark. I can see a gas lamp flickering inside, and the shadows of several people. The scratch of a radio being tuned catches my ear. I freeze just outside the tent as the frequency picks up the familiar chord of a popular violin concerto. I know from experience that it is an enemy propaganda channel.

I remain still, listening to the haunting sound, and I hear Marie's voice suddenly cut across it. "I don't approve," she says, as if it is the continuation of some previous conversation.

There is a snort of derision. A male voice answers, "You don't approve? So what if you don't approve?"

"You said we could do this without getting our own people killed."

"I said that to get you on board," the other voice responds, as if it were the most obvious thing in the world. I decide this must be Commander Paco. "But you've always known the options. We've been negotiating this thing for almost two weeks. If we don't step on it now, someone back in Bava—someone who matters—is going to find out what we're up to and then... well, I'd rather not face a court-martial. Would you?"

I realize I am still standing beside the entrance to the tent. I look over my shoulder to see if I've been spotted, then move around to the side of the tent and hunker down on my haunches, listening. My hands shake.

"No," Marie agrees after a long pause. "But I still don't approve."

"So what?" Paco says. "Have you raised them yet?"

The music suddenly cuts off as the radio is tuned, and then blanks out. It takes me a moment to realize the user has switched to headphones. Some time goes by, and a third voice, male, says in clear, crisp monotone, "Echo-A, receiving, over." Then he says in a normal voice, "I've got them, Paco."

"Good. Tell them we've found Gift Horse."

The radio technician repeats the claim. There is a long silence, and he says, "Confirm. We have Gift Horse location. Over."

There is a long, tense silence. I can barely hear over the pounding in my own ears as I try to get some sort of grasp upon what is going on.

The technician speaks up. "Paco, they want to know

the location."

"Well, where are they?" Paco demands.

It is Marie who answers. "Their Changer says they're camped about half a dozen miles due north of us. My own scouts haven't been able to get their exact location, but we can confirm it if you give us three days."

I see the shadow of Paco shaking his head and pointing at the radio technician. "I'm not giving it three days. Tell them we want amnesty now. Bava is breathing down our necks and we can't hide out here for much longer. Gift Horse is six miles north of our position, but they plan on moving soon. Send a full strike team. We'll give them the location, but then we're coming in. Today."

Gift Horse, I realize, is my own platoon. I am sweating now, trembling from head to foot. The implications are obvious; this isn't a friendly strike force at all. This is an organized desertion. They've stolen supplies and motorbikes, and taken a huge core of Bava's defense militia, and are going over to the other side.

The price of their amnesty, it seems, is the location of my platoon.

And I've given it to them.

I am a wreck now. This is something worse than the heat of battle, worse than flying on Benny's wing. This is betrayal. It takes every instinct—and the reminder that Marie is also a Changer—not to barge into the command tent and try to kill them all where they stand.

These deserters—these traitors—would take me down eventually. There are simply too many for me to fight. But I wonder if it would be better to die now, cutting out their heart, than to allow myself to live knowing of this planned betrayal.

I try to come up with some kind of rationale, but I am unable to think through my rising panic. There is no excuse for this.

I listen, my limbs frozen, unable to will myself into any sort of action as the radio technician relays the message. There is a pregnant pause afterward, and then the technician says to Paco, "They say they'll take care of Gift Horse at first light."

"Our approach?"

"It's been cleared," the technician says.

Paco claps his hands. "Yes! You see that, Marie?" I see his shadow reach across and slap Marie on the shoulder. "We're in."

"So it's done, then?" she asks in a flat voice. I can tell that she is not happy about the betrayal, but it is a distant consideration in the back of my head. At this moment I want nothing more than to gut everyone in that tent.

"It'll be done this afternoon," Paco responds. "Smile, damn it! Get me something to toast with. No, wait. We'll toast at the air base. Get everyone up and ready to move."

I am surprised by the sudden instruction, scrambling to my feet and looking for the way back to my tent. I can hear the creak of Marie's chair, and then the tent flap is thrown back. Marie emerges into the darkness. I attempt to rush farther around the back of the tent, to keep it between us, but I trip on one of the tent cords and fall flat on my face. In my surprise, I cry out.

I realize my mistake the moment the cry leaves my lips. I spring to my feet, turning as Marie rounds the side of the tent. She wears a distracted frown, which grows deeper upon seeing me. "Teado?"

I backpedal. Instinct sends me toward my borrowed tent, as if it is a safe place, but I know that I must run—that I must get out of this place and make it back to Commander Giado. They must be warned.

"Teado, are you all right, I . . ." I can see the moment Marie realizes that I have overheard her conversation with Paco. Her face drains of expression, then her lips are drawn tight. She snatches for her submachine gun, but it is no longer at her hip. In seconds I can see her Changing.

The temptation to Change is strong, almost overwhelming. I want to grapple with her, tear out her throat for this treachery, then do the same to Paco. She begins to move, Changing in midstride, leathery skin and talons ripping through her jacket as she drops to all fours and leaps toward me.

She hits the same tent cord I did, her attack faltering over itself as she stumbles and pulls most of the command tent down with her. I take the opportunity to turn and run.

I am no more graceful in the darkness. I catch the corner of a pallet of supplies with my shoulder, sending myself and dozens of black, hatbox-sized crates scattering to the ground. The sound is impossibly loud in my ears. Between that and Paco's confused shouting as he tries to escape his collapsed tent, I am sure the camp will be fully awake within moments.

My hands scramble for some sort of purchase, and I grip something I know well. It is the handle of a grenade, fallen from the supply crates I have knocked over. I squeeze it tight and regain my feet, my head wrapping around some kind of plan. I am past my borrowed tent and almost to the rows of motorbikes by the time a proper alarm is sounded.

I shove a mechanic out of my way and snatch the best-looking bike of the group, praying it has a full tank of gas. It coughs to life after two kicks, and I rev the engine, spinning the back tire and spraying gravel as I turn around and point toward the camp.

Soldiers emerge sleepily from their tents, confused. Some of them clutch carbines or rifles, but none of them seems to know where to point. The only clear danger is Marie, who has untangled herself from the command tent and is now running toward me, fully Changed.

I pull the pin on the grenade and twist the throttle.

She is quick. I nearly lose control, dipping to one side as her snatching talons rake across my shoulder. I feel the sting of cold on an open wound, and then I am past her, practically flying for the slope that will lead me out of camp. I toss the grenade over my shoulder.

I lean on the throttle as hard as I can and focus, forcing my face to Change. I do not need a scaly, armored body or vicious claws. I only need better night vision, enough to keep me from killing myself as I power up the slope leading from the valley. I am at the crest within moments, and I am somewhat surprised to not hear the bark of gunfire behind me. There are only shouts and searchlights, and I hope that I have caught them unawares enough to make good my escape.

There is a terrible noise, blood rushing to my head and chest, and I am suddenly tumbling head over heels, landing on my back with my vision full of stars as I try to gasp for breath.

I Change almost by instinct, and not a moment too soon. At first I think that Marie has caught me, a flash of talons streaking toward my head. I twist on the ground, turning a shoulder beneath the strike, my own claws ripping upward and shredding a leathery stomach.

I recognize Javiero's Changed form and redouble my efforts, scrambling to my feet. I have only grazed him, but it was enough to drive him on the defensive. I attack quickly, using my superior size to bear down on him, jaws snapping. We skid on the shifting rocks of the mountain trail, exchanging blows, until I am able to slap an open palm against the side of his head. He reels backward, stunned, and I know that I do not have the time to finish him off.

I am half Changed back to human by the time I reach the motorbike. It restarts with a kick, emitting one painful squeal before obeying my turn of the throttle. I careen down the hill blindly, unable to know how closely I am being chased because the valley behind me is still hidden by their Smiling Tom.

I ride with complete disregard for my own life. The trails are narrow and treacherous, and only superhuman luck keeps me from crashing into a boulder or soaring off an embankment into a rocky gorge. I am forced to slow as I round corners and work my way down scree slopes, and at every moment I expect to see the headlights of motorbikes coming up behind me, to feel the dull slap of bullets spinning me off my own motorbike.

I descend from the foothills and make it out on the plain, and it is not until then that I am able to see my pursuers. A line of lights fill the foothills behind me, and I can hear the growl of engines.

I kill my light, risking the darkness, and slow down to navigate the broken ground of the plain. A half a mile later I stop and turn off the engine, hunkering down in one of the many crags crisscrossing the scrubland. Behind me I see that the traitors have stopped just past the foothills, not far from where I killed my light. I can see figures sweeping the hillsides. Soon the engines have been shut off, and a waiting game begins as handheld torches sweep the plain with their flickering beams.

It is not long before I hear a voice calling from farther up in the mountains. It is unintelligible to me, but the putter of motorbike engines fills the night within minutes, and the lights gather and recede back up toward their hideout.

The search, it seems, is called off.

I wonder if it is luck, or fate, or something else. Paco's organized defection seems to have some kind of deadline. I try to think of some way I can disrupt it, and I wish that I had grabbed a whole box of grenades on my way out. It is too late now, and I am forced to hide until long after I see or hear no sign of the enemy.

The first fringe of sunlight appears on the eastern horizon before I pull myself and my stolen motorbike out of the crag and back onto the plain. It takes some effort to get the bike going, but I am soon heading north.

The motorbike allows me to travel much faster than I have on foot, but it still feels like a crawl as I navigate the broken landscape of the Bavares. I am imminently conscious of being so exposed out here, knowing a passing enemy plane will spot me easily in the daylight. I push the worry away. I won't lead an enemy back to my platoon—after all, the enemy is already on their way!

I check behind me every so often, looking for any sign of pursuit. It seems that Paco's men have decided to ignore me, probably content on radioing the enemy, to let their infantry and their Changers deal with me.

My eyes scan the horizon as often as I keep them on the ground ahead of me, and I am knocked from my motorbike from time to time by an unseen rock or shrub. I consider Changing, but know that it will slow my progress even further. I become more bruised and beaten with each fall. I become conscious of my new clothes, shredded from my brief, Changed fight with Javiero, and the chill wind blowing through them as I ride. My eyes pinch against the dust and the wind, and against my own exhaustion.

Every physical worry is relegated to a mere whisper in the back of my head as I spot a dust cloud to my east. It rises quickly, drawing closer, producing a panic in my chest that is impossible to control.

The cloud is coming on hard from the direction of the old enemy air base. I stop on a slight rise long enough to squint toward it, trying to make out some of the movement. I think that I see motorbikes and jeeps. They bounce across the terrain, straight toward my platoon's hidden canyon.

This must be the enemy strike force tasked to eradicate Gift Horse—the price paid by Paco and Marie and the rest of the traitors to secure their amnesty.

The next fall undoes me. The front tire of my motorbike catches in a rut and bends, rendering the bike unusable. I lose precious minutes attempting to bend it back, and then give up and continue on foot.

I estimate that I am three miles from my platoon. I begin to run, forcing my ragged body across the plains, watching helplessly as the dust cloud grows larger. On my motorbike I might have beaten them to the canyon and given my friends fair warning to stand and fight—or even Bellara the chance to use her illusions to cover our withdrawal deeper into the mountains.

It's easy to see that the enemy will reach the canyon before me. I hope against hope that my earlier fears—that my platoon will have stripped the captured cargo plane and changed locations—have come true, and that the enemy's search for them will be fruitless.

I whisper that, if they are still there, they have a proper guard set up, and will mount a defense.

I am sick in the pit of my stomach as the cloud continues to grow. I estimate they have forty men. Then sixty. Then eighty. I am assaulted by fear for my friends. I think of Giado, hopeless and angry; of Aleta's optimism over her miserable coffee, and Selvie's work on our endlessly breaking motorbikes. I think of Bellara and her illusions, and I hope that at the end she will save herself.

But I know Bellara will be unable to abandon her brother, even if she could bring herself to leave the others.

Despite my best efforts, my body begins to slow. My limbs are heavy, my muscles weak. I Change, dropping to all fours, loping through the brush. The Change gives me some extra strength, but I can feel my weakness even here from within my sorcery. It is not enough, and despair takes me.

Even if I reach my friends at the same time as the enemy, I will make little difference. A Changer can take out a squad, even a whole platoon with the proper amount of surprise and planning. But they'll see me coming, and I will be even weaker than I am now.

I consider just giving up, lying down in a ditch until night falls, and then making my way into the mountains. I can return to Bava and tell the tale of these traitors.

Or I can simply disappear, letting myself go far from the guns and bombs and sorcery, where I can die on my own terms. It is a sobering thought, a tempting one, but some hidden strength keeps me moving. If I am to die, I will die with my friends.

I stop for a rest and hazard a sweep of the Bavares, only to spot another cloud to my southeast. I assume it is the traitors, heading to the old enemy air base in order to finalize their amnesty. They form a long convoy of motorbikes that stretches for a mile or more across the plains, and I silently curse them.

I bark a laugh, the laugh of a desperate man, realizing I am caught between two enemy convoys and the unforgiving mountains. In a brief moment I am overcome with a feeling that everything will be all right. I am weightless, worriless. Distantly, I realize that it is an adrenaline-fueled acceptance of death.

I am not sure how long I stand, facing the sun, eyes unfocused, before the sudden shock of an explosion nearly knocks me off my feet.

I am startled back to reality, my ears full of noise. Screams echo off the mountains, and there is the immediate, demanding bark of small arms fire. The enemy convoy, almost two miles away and nearly into the foothills, has erupted into chaos.

I stand dumbfounded for several moments as I try to make sense of it all. An explosion rips apart an enemy jeep, sending bodies flying. Another erupts nearby, knocking one man off his motorcycle. I begin to move again, forcing myself forward at a limping run.

The enemy convoy falls apart, fanning across the plain as men abandon motorcycles and jeeps. I imagine myself among them, and can practically hear the conflicting orders as they try to make something of the chaos. Men fall as if suddenly pushed over by a stiff wind, and as I grow closer I can see the tiny, erupting geysers of sand from bullets hitting the ground.

I realize that my platoon is fighting back. Selvie probably has our machine gun up in the entrance to the valley, while Aleta hides in the mountains with her rifle. Bellara has them all hidden with her sorcery. I cannot determine the source of the explosions.

I laugh again, and this time I can hear the joyful hysteria in the sound. Traitorous bastards notwithstanding, my friends will not go down without a fight. They have the best Smiling Tom left in Bava, and the grittiest guerillas in the whole Bavares.

The enemy is fighting an invisible foe, but their numbers begin to quickly show. They knew we have a Smiling Tom, and they have brought their own wizards. I see two Changers emerge from the ruins of a jeep, their bodies gnarled, skin stained with grit and ash, but otherwise unharmed. They charge into the foothills, ignoring lines of machine gun and carbine fire.

The enemy infantry follows them, moving with trained precision, running forward under covering fire and sweeping the mountainside with bullets.

The first hint that something has gone wrong is that I can suddenly hear the sound of a single-engine plane overhead. I look around for the source, wondering if the enemy has brought fighter support, only to see Benny suddenly pop into existence above the enemy forces. I watch as Rodrigo hurls a grenade out of the cockpit and track its movement down to the ground, where it explodes among a squad of enemy infantry.

I am less than a mile away now, and I watch as the enemy turns their carbines and submachine guns on Rodrigo. Benny suddenly dips and spins, then tries to climb to get out of range of the enemy.

I am close enough now to hear the cough of the engine, and then a long, mechanical whine. Benny belches a single cloud of black smoke, then slowly arcs to one side and begins to descend in a barely controlled fall. I push myself harder, faster, my eyes wide as I watch the continued trace of enemy gunfire follow Rodrigo toward the ground.

The mouth of our canyon appears next, coming into sudden clarity where there was once a mountainside, and I realize that something has happened to Bellara to make her illusions fail. I think of the Changers I saw rushing ahead and swallow a sob. I am sprinting now, gathering every last reserve of strength in a last-ditch effort to reach my friends before they are wiped out.

I reach the blackened earth and ruined trail of destruction that marks where Benny went down. A moment of indecision halts me as I watch enemy soldiers take and hold the mouth of the canyon up ahead, then I head the opposite direction to follow the charred ground and burning shrubs to what remains of Benny.

The old fighter is riddled with bullets, landing gear sheared off by the harsh terrain. Smoke pours from her engine compartment, flames licking at the propeller. Rodrigo sits still in the cockpit, slumped over the stick. I ignore the heat and the smoke, blinking tears from my eyes as I shear the metal side off the cockpit with my talons and then carefully drag Rodrigo from the wreck. His chest and legs are covered with blood, and a single cough is all that tells me he is still alive.

I carry him far from the danger of the wreckage and lay him on his side, then force myself to abandon him, resuming my trip toward the canyon. I say a word for Benny and her broken hulk, and I weep for Rodrigo as I run, knowing he will be dead by the time I can return.

I reach the edge of the small battlefield where a jeep lies on its side, destroyed by one of Rodrigo's grenades and upended by enemy soldiers to use for cover. A medic attends to a trio of wounded behind the cover.

In my pain and fury I kill all four of them. I make it quick, messy. My talons are slick with gore as I stalk up the slope, falling upon every enemy soldier that I see. Most are already wounded, or hiding until they are certain that their allies have secured the mountainside up ahead. A distant part of me remembers a time when they told us to spare the enemy wounded, but that was so long ago I barely remember it.

The sound of gunfire has all but abated. I can hear shouting, and wonder absently if it is a demand for surrender, or commands being issued to flush the rest of the canyon. I can still see enemy soldiers moving around in the mouth of the canyon so I know they have won.

I sob silently as I kill, wishing that someone would turn around and raise the alarm, that a hail of gunfire would overwhelm me, putting an end to the entirety of my little platoon of guerrillas. But the enemy is too focused on the canyon, and those that notice me only do so just before my claws slash at their chests and my teeth can open their throats.

I can taste nothing but the salty iron of blood and my own, all-too-human bile. I begin to ignore the enemy wounded. Some of them try to shout a warning to their comrades as they see me pass, but the enemy's blood is still up, and the occasional carbine shot tells me that there is still something going on in the canyon.

Four soldiers hunker just outside the canyon. One sees me, raising the alarm. I sprint across the open, rocky ground between us. A carbine blast hits me point-blank in the cheek, spinning me around. The side of my face goes numb and I lash out, catching a handful of cloth and flesh and tearing blindly. The bark of carbines and pistols makes my head spin, and I silence them with four well-placed swipes and continue on into the canyon.

My ears ring, and everything I hear seems to come to me from within a dream. I stand upright, my big, Changed shoulders hunched, and limp into the mouth of the canyon. I glance up to Bellara's little cave up above the scree and see the sun playing across it. I think that it must be very warm and comforting in that spot.

Bodies lie scattered all over, and the canyon walls are nicked and chipped by gunfire. More of the bodies belong to them than they do to us. I immediately spot the corpses of my friends.

Garcia lies behind our machine gun, both man and gun mangled by a grenade. He's an old man, who used to take pride in his looks and wax poetic over sandwiches with ingredients I have never seen in my lifetime. Now his cracked, handsome face is barely recognizable.

Natal is slumped over a boulder, carbine in her hands, her body still and bloody. Her lover, Donilo, lies at her feet, hands outstretched, riddled with submachine gun fire as he reaches for her.

Commander Giado lies splayed in the middle of the

camp. He is surrounded by enemy corpses and grips two pistols, both of them spent, his body a mangled mess. He has been dispatched by a shot to the head, as if he refused to die from a dozen other wounds.

I am exhausted. Tears streak my bloody, smoke-stained cheeks and I rock unsteadily on my feet. I have nothing left to give, and each step is as if over a mountain. Through my hazy vision I see a cluster of enemy troops, carbines hanging from their shoulders, and my breath catches in my throat as I see their prize.

They stand around a small group of kneeling figures. Selvie's shirt is covered in more blood splotches than I can count. Bellara stares at the dirt, expressionless, her hand clutching at a bloody shoulder. Our medic, Harado, is unwounded, but he has never been a fighter. Vicente is slumped face-first in the dirt, trembling, clutching his stomach. They even have Aleta, her pretty face torn across the right cheek and bleeding profusely.

Someone, perhaps the leader of this expedition, is asking Aleta a question. She stares over his shoulder, proudly, refusing to answer. He backhands her hard enough to knock her on her side, but she crawls back to her knees and resumes her stubborn stare.

I can feel the fury churning in my belly. I beg my body to give me something else with which to fight. I search deep inside, trying to well up the strength to dash forward, but it is like dipping a bucket in an empty well, and it is all I can do to limp toward the small group with my gnarled, Changed knuckles dragging on the ground.

Their commander asks Aleta another question. It is more forceful, demanding. She opens her mouth, then stops. I see her eyes land upon me. They widen, fearful, and her face seems to change. The stubbornness melts away, and she slumps inwardly, as if she has given up the fight.

The enemy commander laughs and leans toward her, repeating his questions.

Her lips tighten, and she spits at him. The enemy commander reels back, blood spattering his face and clean uniform. He shouts, kicking her in the stomach, then draws his pistol.

I want to ask her what she is doing. I silently beg her to stop fighting—to surrender and live through this thing. Selvie and Harado attempt to gain their feet. My friends scream at the enemy commander, who waves his pistol under their noses and then puts the barrel against Aleta's forehead.

She meets my eyes, and I realize with startling clarity that she is buying me time. She sees that I am spent, and must know from my state that I have no strength. And yet she still has faith to try and gain me the time I need to sneak up on these bastards.

The enemy commander shouts in Aleta's ear, shoving

the pistol hard against her forehead. She leans into it, looking him in the eyes, then turning her head toward me. She smiles at me at the enemy commander pulls the trigger, and the bullet snuffs out her life.

It is the strength I need. I surge forward, that smile frozen in my mind as my steps become quick and forceful.

The enemy's men are too busy beating my friends with the stocks of their carbines to see me coming. I do not kill the commander. I open his stomach before he can scream, and then I turn on his men.

There are around a dozen enemies left. I know that two of them are Changers, but I do not know which they are. I slash and cut, moving as quickly as I dare. My vision is a haze, my hearing almost nonexistent. Only the image of Aleta's smile floating in my head keeps me going as I bury my talons in a stomach, open a throat with my claws, and bite the stock of a carbine in two as it is thrust in my face.

A pistol shot goes off under my elbow, and I tear off the arm of the man holding the weapon. A shotgun blast to the base of my spine drives me to my knees, and I turn to take another blast in the chest. I recover and maul the woman holding the shotgun before she can reload, and I leap for a man shoving a new clip into his machine pistol.

The enemy Changer tackles me from the side. He is smaller than me, but he is relatively fresh, and I feel his talons tear into my shoulders as we wrestle in the dust. I lean into him, letting the talons tear deeper, and bite off his face with two snaps of my jaw.

I leave him screaming and writhing to finish off his comrades. Three more enemy soldiers empty their weapons into me, the hot shot hitting my body like stinging nettles on the end of a blackjack. Two die quickly. One tries to run, and is shot in the back by Selvie, who has recovered a pistol from the enemy commander.

I stumble to one side, my Changed body slick with blood—my own and that of my enemies. My legs give out and I fall to my knees. I am barely conscious as the remaining members of my platoon re-arm themselves and regain their feet. I don't even have the energy to wince at the seven blasts from the shotgun it takes to put down the enemy Changer, or feel satisfaction when Selvie executes the commander I disemboweled.

I feel someone touch me and I jerk around, almost snagging Bellara with my claws. She gives me a moment to recognize her before coming closer. She puts her hands on my cheeks and looks me in the eyes, and calls for Harado.

"Where is the other Changer?" I ask. My voice is barely audible through the twisted nature of my Changed form, and my own weakness.

"Garcia killed him with the machine gun," Bellara responds.

Killed by a machine gun. Hardly able to call himself

a Changer. I try to chuckle, but it comes out as a gurgle. Harado tells me to lie down. I ignore him, and make Bellara help me to my feet.

I remain standing, ostensibly a guard as Selvie and Harado sweep the canyon, though I doubt I could move if even a single enemy appeared to attack me. They find three more of our platoon still holed up in the caves, and I can see the fear and wonder in their eyes as they come out to see the destruction that has been wrought.

I remain Changed, fearful that my wounds would kill me on the spot if I become human again. Bellara remains at my side, clutching my leathery, blood-slick hand. She talks to me in a quiet voice.

"We thought you died from the fall out of the cargo plane," she tells me. "But Rodrigo scouted the next day, and claims he saw you hiding in a valley. We've been waiting for you to return ever since."

I try not to cry at the news that they waited for me, and I stay quiet with the terrible knowledge that their waiting got most of them killed. I try to look past the carnage, noting the crates of supplies stacked in the mouth of the caves, and tell myself that they were able to eat like kings for the last week of their lives.

"Rodrigo . . ." I manage.

"I know," Bellara says, her face somber. "I saw Benny go down."

I want to tell her that he was still alive when I left him, that she should send someone down to check on him, but I know that he is already dead, and the plain outside our canyon is dangerous. Telling her he might be alive would be a cruelty.

Besides, there is no one to send. Everyone is wounded—I see now that even Harado's hand has been hurt by shrapnel—and Selvie's venture to the mouth of our canyon ends with a report that there is still movement down in the foothills. I am unable to give them any guess as to the number of enemy wounded I left alive, or if there was a squad or two that I missed.

Bellara reveals that she dropped her illusions when she took a bullet in the shoulder, and was unable to get them back up because a Changer took her captive. They singled her out, wanted her alive. I can hear the catch in her throat as she says this, though her expression remains unchanged. I put my grotesque head on her shoulder and close my eyes, hoping she takes it as some sign of comfort.

I tell them of Paco's defection and the loss of so many of our soldiers to the enemy amnesty. I tell them I gave away our position, and repeat myself so that they can mete out any judgment they see fit. A third repetition passes without comment, and I feel hollow inside. They do not judge me. They will not judge me.

Selvie ignores her wounds and begins to organize a retreat farther into the mountains. We must regroup, heal, and return to Bava, she says. We must tell them what happened here.

Bellara gently leaves my side. She winks from existence a dozen paces away, and I try to call out for her, but I have no strength. Each pain reemerges with movement. I wonder if I will have to remain Changed for weeks before I am healthy enough to be human again. Despite Harado's bandages, I have lost a great deal of blood.

I wonder if I am dying, and find it curious that I don't dwell on my coming death. I think that perhaps no one wishes to face their own mortality. Perhaps self-denial is the last pleasure a soldier feels.

I do not die, though the hours tick by. My surviving friends move the bodies and attend to our wounded. Their wounded are shoved to one side and forgotten, or forced at gunpoint to help Selvie inventory what we will need to retreat into the mountains. Bellara returns, and reports that there are only a handful of the enemy left able to fight, and they have concerned themselves with trying to repair one of their jeeps. She also reports motorbikes on the eastern horizon.

I try to get myself to move at that news. I remind them of Paco's desertion, and that the enemy still has more men. Selvie seems to be the only one with the strength to keep moving, and insists we arm ourselves. The enemy wounded are forced into the mouth of the canyon, where their presence will foul enemy grenades and gunfire.

I soon hear the sound of the motorbikes. By the pitch of the engines I guess they are ours, which means Paco and his cronies have come to finish the job. Bellara tells me to relax, and gives me a carbine even though my Changed fingers are too big for the guard. We hunker down behind a boulder and wait. I close my eyes, trying to gather my strength for one last fight.

I will die ripping Paco's throat out, or in the attempt.

The sound of the motorbikes comes almost to the very entrance of the canyon before cutting out. I can hear many voices. There is shouting between the enemy wounded and these new arrivals, and several minutes pass before a figure appears in the mouth of the canyon.

I recognize Marie. She is in her human form, her sub-machine gun slung under her arm. She surveys the carnage, head held high, nodding to herself. "Friendly!" she shouts.

"Another step and I will kill you," Bellara replies. She sits beside me, and I can tell the blood loss has taken a lot out of her. I wonder if she can even hit a stationary target.

Marie snorts. "Don't be stupid," she says. "We're from Bava."

"We know about the amnesty," Selvie responds. She is along the opposite canyon wall, covering Bellara and myself with a rifle.

Marie opens her mouth, then shuts it again. Her eyes fall on me and she shakes her head in disbelief. I want to taunt her, to tell her the ambush did not work, and that her new friends will think she has betrayed them, and that her amnesty will not be honored. I want to tell her she is a traitor, and I want to kill her with my own two hands.

Slowly, carefully, Marie takes the submachine gun off her shoulder and sets it on the ground. She takes a few cautious steps forward.

"She's a Changer," I tell Bellara. "Don't let her get closer."

Bellara fires a warning shot that ricochets off the stones at Marie's feet. I'm not so sure it was meant to be a warning shot, but she reloads and holds her fire.

"We just want to talk," Marie insists. I am impressed at her ability to remain calm. My own blood is racing, and I feel we are on the cusp of a terrible last stand, with Marie's Changer and infantry rushing into the canyon while we all slaughter each other.

"I don't trust you," I croak.

"Teado, you don't know what's going on. Come here and speak to me."

I decide not to tell her that I am unable to move. I look across the canyon to Selvie, who shakes her head. We have no way out; we have missed our chance at a safe retreat. I wonder if we can take Marie captive, but dismiss the thought. She would kill us all in close quarters.

Her weapon still on Marie, Bellara stands up from behind cover and walks across the canyon. I can hear a whispered consultation with Selvie and the others, and then she returns to me.

"What is happening?" I ask.

Bellara doesn't respond. I can see Selvie setting down her pistol. She comes out of hiding and heads toward Marie. "We're going to talk," Bellara finally answers.

"Don't trust her," I repeat.

Bellara is tight-lipped.

"I'm sorry," I say.

"For what?" Bellara asks. We both watch Selvie cautiously cross the corpse-ridden ground.

"For everything. For falling out of the cargo plane. For stumbling on those traitors, and telling them our location. I'm sorry I won't get to see you dance." The words tumble out, and I'm not sure what part of me is speaking. I can barely move my lips.

"Don't be a fool," Bellara says. "We'll get out of this." I can tell she does not believe it.

Selvie and Marie stand several paces apart. Selvie is tensed to run. Marie seems relaxed. They speak for minutes, and Selvie shakes her head each time Marie gestures. The gesturing becomes more desperate, until at long last Selvie gives a tired nod. She follows Marie and both figures disappear from view.

"It's a trap!" I say, trying to struggle to my feet. Bellara holds me down, though I am so much bigger and stronger. I try not to pass out from the effort of fighting her, until sweat covers my face. Only Selvie's reappearance takes the fight out of me.

Selvie jogs back into camp, her face animated. She is followed at a cautious distance by Marie, and several soldiers behind her. They are all armed, and one of those soldiers is Martin, her cousin. My hair stands on end.

"Put your weapons down!" Selvie orders. "They are friendlies. Everyone put your weapons down!"

This time Bellara isn't able to keep me down. I surge to my feet. "No! It's a trick, don't let them . . ."

Selvie throws herself toward me. "Teado, you must calm down. It isn't a trick!"

Before anyone can make sense of the confusion, Marie and her men are among us. My friends are disarmed, and Marie crosses the distance to stand beside Selvie. She looks down at me with what I take as a look of arrogant pity. I summon all my reserves and take a swipe at her.

Martin Changes before my blow can land. He catches my arm and clamps me by the shoulders, wrestling me into submission with a distressingly small amount of effort. Several soldiers gather around me and, despite my calls for Selvie and Bellara not to be tricked, I am forced from my hiding spot.

They half carry, half drag me to the mouth of the canyon. I can see Benny still smoking off on the plains, and the destruction left in the wake of the ambush, battle, and my own counterattack. There are about forty new motorbikes down beyond the runway, and I see Marie's men combing the battlefield. Despite their betrayal, they are still wearing jackets with the Bava militia patch on the shoulder.

A gunshot rings out on the plain. Another follows it. There is a scream, and I look to see that Marie's men are executing the enemy wounded.

I turn to look over my shoulder, confused, and find Marie standing beside me. She has a satisfied look on her face.

In the distance, a tall plume of smoke rises from the enemy air base.

"What has happened?" I ask Marie—the last words I am able to speak before consciousness finally fails me.

———

The nurses tell me that I am in a hospital in Bava. It does not look like a hospital—the walls are too clean, the ceiling is intact, and the lights do not flicker. I am in a single room, and it feels tiny and isolated compared to the rows of wounded I have seen in other hospitals. They claim it is a hospital for very important people, and that it is in the southeast corner of Bava where it was spared the worst of the bombing.

I do not know whether to believe them. I remember the overheard conversation between Paco and Marie, and the fight, and the bodies of my friends. I feel as if I cannot trust anything, even my own senses.

I do not feel like a very important person.

I am human again. My body is covered in cuts and bruises, and I have broken an arm and a wrist, but I seem to have avoided any permanent damage.

I have vague memories of being carried, then transported by car, then by plane, and once again by car. The nurses speak my language. They seem far too kind. I wonder if this is some kind of trick, and demand to see Selvie and Bellara. The nurses claim not to know either of those names.

I am too worn out, my body still weak from blood loss and starvation, to fight them. I sleep through the night, and wake again to daylight. A figure sits beside my bed, and at first I take him for a nurse.

I tell myself, upon a second glance, that my eyes are playing tricks on me. Rodrigo sits in a rickety wheelchair. His head and chest are wrapped in white bandages, and his arm is in a sling, but his eyes are open, staring at the pages of a book clutched in one hand.

I must make some kind of noise, because he turns toward

me and his thin face lights up. "Teado!" he says. "They told me you were awake, but I did not dare to hope."

I lick my lips, and try to remember what Bellara has told me about seeing through illusions. *This* is a trick. It has to be. Rodrigo was barely alive when I pulled him from Benny's wreck. I reach out, and Rodrigo puts aside his book to take my hand in his, then kisses my knuckles. It sounds like Rodrigo. It feels like Rodrigo. It acts like Rodrigo.

"You're alive?" is all I can manage.

"I am at that, my friend," he responds with gusto. "They tell me that a Changer pulled me from the wreckage, so there is someone out there who I owe a debt, but . . ." He makes a gesture as if this mysterious wizard has disappeared into thin air. His smile is lopsided, and disappears for a moment. "Benny, I'm afraid, did not survive the crash."

I want to reach across and slap him for mentioning that machine before our friends, but I know it is just in his nature. "Your wounds?" I ask.

He squeezes my hand and pulls back. "Paralyzed from the waist down," he says, slapping one thigh. "An enemy bullet. These useless hunks of meat will never operate the pedals again."

I let out a soft sigh. "Rod—"

"No, no," he cuts me off, as if I am his little sister. "I will not be defeated by a mere bullet. Selvie says she can create a mechanism that will let me operate the flaps with my elbows. I will fly again, or my name is not Rodrigo." He rolls his eyes at my stricken expression. "Don't be such a downer. We are alive, my friend, and that is what is important."

I can see a pain in his eyes, though he hides it well. I am surprised that his optimism has survived the crash, but grateful for it. "Where are we?" I ask.

"In Bava," he answers. "One of those officers' hospitals."

"How did we end up here?"

Rodrigo's face sours. "You met Marie?"

I bristle at the name, the betrayal still hot in my memory. "I did."

"She is an old lover of mine. Years ago, a torrid affair," he says, waving it off, "but her father is a general. Seems she pulled some strings."

"So we have you to thank for this?"

"Me?" he scoffs. "I'm surprised I made it back in one piece. Our last separation was not a pleasant one. No, it turns out she's taken a shine to you."

I feel like I should be flattered. "She betrayed us," I say bluntly.

Rodrigo's face is somber. "Let it go," he says seriously.

"How?"

"Not *how*," a voice interrupts. "That is your own problem. *Why* might be a better question." Marie stands in the doorway. She is both prettier and older than I first expected. Her hair has been freshly cut and her uniform is clean and sharp. Despite our location, she wears a pistol at her belt.

I stiffen. Rodrigo turns white and ducks his head. "I should go."

"Please do," Marie says.

"No, stay," I utter at the same time.

Rodrigo wheels his chair, one-handed, past Marie. She makes no move to help him though it is clear the motion is very painful. She watches him go coldly, then turns back to me.

"You and I should talk," she says, closing the door. I remain tight-lipped, stubborn. She doesn't seem to care. Rodrigo says she's taken a shine to me, but there is absolutely no indication in her demeanor. "You need to forget what happened up in the mountains."

"I see no reason to."

"The operation was sanctioned by high command."

"What operation?" I ask. I've been putting the pieces together in my head, and I think I have a pretty good idea by now, but I want to be sure.

Marie pulls a chair over beside my bed and sits down. She is still distant, cold, but I sense this is meant as a gesture of trust between us. I don't buy it. She says, "For five months, Commander Paco and I have been organizing a false mass-defection. It has been a colossal effort of misinformation that included fooling some of our own generals. It was an enormous risk, but we desperately needed that air base intact."

"You could have told us about it," I say. "You could have given us a part to play."

"We couldn't find you."

"We got radio communications from you all the time! And Rodrigo was in Bava almost every other week!"

"The radio was too risky, and Paco thinks that Rodrigo is a loose-lipped fool. Besides, Gift Horse had to look genuine. If we gave you the chance to set up an ambush it might have tipped off the enemy before we had taken their base."

Gift Horse. A code name for handing my platoon over to the enemy as a distraction. It is a bitter pill.

"You got most of my platoon killed."

"And saved almost all of the strike force in the process. It was a distasteful strategy, but I would do it again in an instant."

"Is that supposed to make me feel better?" I demand.

"Not in the least." She lowers her voice until her tone is almost gentle. "Teado, your friends did not die for nothing. I'm sorry it had to happen like it did."

"I won't forget it."

"Why not? This is war. We forget things which are inconvenient to remember. Just like I will forget the grenade I dove on when you attacked a government strike force." She unbuttons the front of her shirt and pulls it down. Her chest is crisscrossed with week-old scars, the skin barely beginning to heal. I remember the grenade I tossed over my shoulder during my mad scramble to escape Paco's camp.

She buttons her shirt back up. "No one died," she says. "I was Changed at the time so it didn't do any permanent damage, but Paco still wanted you court-martialed."

I feel a cold sweat break out on the back of my neck and almost laugh. After all this, will I get shot by my own side?

"I won't allow it to happen," she continues. "Unfortunately, I had to paint you as a hero to get high command to ignore the whole thing. It wasn't hard. With no warning your platoon almost destroyed an enemy strike force five times your number. And you ... well, that was a pretty bit of fighting."

"A hero, huh? Am I supposed to be grateful?" I am taken aback, my breast swelling with conflicting emotions.

She snorts. "Yes, in fact. You are. But I'll give you a few weeks to come around to it." She stands up, adjusting her uniform and giving me a tight-lipped smile. "In the meantime, I expect you to enjoy the hospitality here and get better. The remnants of your platoon are expected to be healed and ready for duty within eight weeks."

This declaration is like a punch to the gut. I should

have expected it, but . . . "You're going to split us up?" After all we've been through, I don't think I can bear to be assigned to a whole new platoon.

Marie shakes her head. "No. You'll be joining my platoon."

More conflicting emotions. "Even Bellara?" I can't imagine that anyone in the military command would allow two Changers and a Smiling Tom in a single platoon.

"Even Bellara," Marie confirms. "I have use for such an experienced group. I'll make sure you don't go to waste. That is, if the war is still going once you've healed."

I am looking at the wall now, feeling distant and confused, but this last sentence brings my head around. "What do you mean, if the war is still going?"

Marie comes around to the other side of the bed. Her face draws close to mine, and I see suddenly that the coldness is a mask. Her expression softens, her eyes mellowing. "I don't believe in half measures, Teado. I agreed to that mission, including Gift Horse, because the stakes are higher than they've ever been. We may have ended the war."

My breath catches in my throat. I am instantly suspicious, because I've heard promises of peace since I was a child. "From the capture of one base?" I ask.

"It was a vital piece of the enemy's attack corridor in this region." Marie glances toward the door, and her voice is merely a whisper. "No one wants war anymore, Teado. The capture of the air base shows we still have some bite, and that gives us leverage. Talks have already begun." She stands up, clearing her throat. "But you haven't heard any of that."

I do not respond. I am stunned. Peace, in my lifetime? Could it really be possible? I want to ask more questions, but Marie exits as quickly as she arrived. I am left open-mouthed, flapping like a fish, when Bellara enters the room.

It seems like she's been waiting for Marie to leave. She crosses to my bedside and immediately snatches me into a fierce hug. I feel a terrible pinch in my wrist and try not to squeal from the pain. She finally lets me go and pulls back. Her eyes are sad, but she smiles and kisses my cheeks, then my lips.

"What was that for?" I ask.

"For saving Rodrigo," she replies. "And me, and Selvie, and everyone else."

I swallow. "I couldn't save everyone."

"You saved the ones you could."

There is an awkward silence, and I feel like I should say something. Nothing comes to mind. I feel the knot between my shoulders begin to fade, realizing that Bellara has given me an absolution that I didn't know I sought. I take a deep breath, but Bellara shakes her head. She closes the door, and returns to me, climbing into the tiny hospital bed. The movement brings pain.

I do not object.

"What are . . . ?" I begin to ask.

She puts a finger against my lips and lays her head on my shoulder. We lie quietly for several minutes and I am about to speak again when I smell something strange.

It takes me a few moments to place the scent. It smells of spring wildflowers in the lower Bavares, the scent of soil laid bare to the world after the melting of the snow. I hear birdsong, startling me, and when I look for the source of the sound I am no longer in a hospital in Bava. I lie on a grassy, lowland field, the dark green of wild pastures splashed with the brilliant colors of spring spread out for as far as the eye can see. A brook bubbles nearby.

My bed is now a patterned sheet laid on the dewy grass. There is a picnic basket at our feet.

I look down at Bellara. Her head is still on my chest, her eyes closed. I know this is an illusion, but it feels so real I want to cry. Bits of propaganda float through my head—admonitions against wasting sorcery on anything but the war effort. I discard them and put my good arm around Bellara, and allow myself to fade to sleep with dreams of peace.

About the Author

Photograph by Emily Bischoff

BRIAN MCCLELLAN is an American epic fantasy author from Cleveland, Ohio. He is known for his acclaimed Powder Mage universe and essays on the life and business of being a writer. Brian now lives on the side of a mountain in Utah with his wife, Michele, where he writes books and nurses a crippling video game addiction.

TOR·COM

Science fiction. Fantasy. The universe.

And related subjects.

*

More than just a publisher's website, *Tor.com*
is a venue for **original fiction, comics,** and
discussion of the entire field of SF and fantasy,
in all media and from all sources. Visit our site
today — and join the conversation yourself.